aUNT BeLLe'S BeaCH

To Busybodies everywhere

Thanks to
Ellen and Laura Gellis
Deborah Gould, Alan Finkelstein,
Marjorie Forte and Mameve Medwed

Library of Congress Cataloging in Publication Data was not available in time for
the publication of this book, but can be obtained from the Library of Congress.
Aunt Belle's Beach. ISBN 0-688-11628-0 — ISBN 0-688-11629-9 (lib. bdg.).
Library of Congress Catalog Card Number: 93-85980.

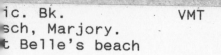

MARJORY WUNSCH

AUNT BELLE'S BEACH

LOTHROP, Lee & Shepard Books   New York

unt Belle found her favorite patch of sand and shook her beach chair open with a loud thwack.

"There, Rosa," she said, tying a huge balloon to the back of her chair. "So you'll always know where to find me."

"Why don't you keep your robe on today?" Rosa suggested. "So you won't get a sunburn." But it didn't do any good.

"I think I'll catch a few rays," said Aunt Belle. She wiggled out of her beach robe, then twirled around so Rosa could admire her new bathing suit.

Rosa built a sandcastle. Aunt Belle acted as if she owned the beach. "You there," she shouted. "How about slam-dunking that candy wrapper into the litter basket?…Hey, little girl at the shower! Are you taking the whole beach home with you? Better give yourself a good rinse!"

"Time for our beach walk," Aunt Belle announced. She marched down to the shore. "Don't swim too soon after you eat," she warned picnickers. "Use sunscreen number fifteen," she cautioned two sunbathers.

Rosa shuffled along behind her. By the time they reached the jetty, her cheeks were hot, and it wasn't from the sun.

"Young man," shouted Belle. "You're not supposed to be out there. Don't you know the rules?"

The man seemed not to hear. Aunt Belle screamed louder. "*Young man.* You're not *supposed* to be out there. Don't you know the rules?"

This time the man turned. A whistle hung around his neck. He held a large sign: KEEP OFF THE ROCKS! He was the lifeguard! "Oops," murmured Aunt Belle. Rosa dropped to the ground in a frantic search for hermit crabs.

As Aunt Belle flipped through a magazine, Rosa worked on her sandcastle. For a while, the only sound was Aunt Belle's balloon, flapping in the breeze. But the calm didn't last long.

"Swim time!" sang Aunt Belle. "Aren't you going to warm up with me, Rosa—do a few jumping jacks?"

Aunt Belle breathed deeply, touched her toes five times, and did twenty jumping jacks. Rosa was sure the whole beach was staring.

Rosa waded up to her ankles and slowly wet her arms and legs. Aunt Belle plunged right in. When Rosa looked around, she had disappeared. There were lots of people in the water— even the lifeguard with his swimming class. But no Aunt Belle.

"All right, everybody. Let's see some serious back-floating," said the lifeguard.

No one in the class could do the back-float. The children began to fidget. Rosa searched for Aunt Belle as the lifeguard gave another demonstration. His class was still confused.

They were even more puzzled when a small flowered island suddenly appeared. The island grew bigger and bumpier. Aunt Belle had surfaced.

"How ya doin'?" she greeted the lifeguard as she waved to Rosa.

"Uh, fine, thanks," he answered, then tried to get on with his lesson. "Okay, kids," he shouted, "back to the back-float!"

"Don't mind me," said Aunt Belle. She watched as eight children flung themselves backward, looked up at the sky, then began to splutter and sink.

"Tsk, tsk, tsk," said Aunt Belle. "Hold on, everyone. I'll be right back."

The lifeguard scowled.

Aunt Belle rushed to her chair, untied the balloon, then hurried back to the swimming class. She tied the balloon around her waist.

"Watch!" said Aunt Belle, relaxing into a back-float. "Just pretend a huge balloon is attached to your belly button, and that balloon is pulling you up, up, up to the sky."

The children began to giggle and scream.

"Thank you, lady," snapped the lifeguard. "But *I'll* teach this class if you don't mind."

Aunt Belle shrugged and walked back to her chair.

"If you lie down right here," said Rosa, "I can bury your feet in the sand."

"Sure, honey," Aunt Belle agreed. She yawned, rolled a beach towel into a pillow, and lay down. In no time at all, she was snoring.

Rosa buried Aunt Belle's feet, then her legs, then her belly, then her chest, till she looked like a range of sandy mountains. As she stepped back to admire her work, she heard a sniffle behind her.

"I'm lost!" cried a small boy. "I want my mommy!"

Aunt Belle's eyes popped open. The mountains of sand began to slip and slide. Like an earthquake, she sprang into action.

"Don't worry, dearie," Aunt Belle told the frightened boy. "We'll find your mommy. Just come with me. What did you say your name was?"

"Oliver," blubbered the little boy.

Aunt Belle set out with Oliver. Rosa could still hear his sobs. They reminded her of the time she got lost in the supermarket.

Rosa ran to the lifeguard's empty chair and found his megaphone. Would he get mad if she touched his things? She looked back at Oliver. Then she picked up the megaphone. Sometimes you just *had* to be a busybody.

With a Belle-like voice, Rosa boomed, "Attention, please! Attention, please! We have a lost boy named Oliver who wants his mother. Would Oliver's mother please come to the lifeguard's chair. Thank you."

Aunt Belle and Oliver rushed back to Rosa. "What a good idea!" said Aunt Belle. Then she stared down the beach. Rosa stared with her. Oliver sniffled.

Finally a frantic woman came racing toward them. "I'm coming, Oliver," she called.

"Thank you so much," said Oliver's mother as she gave him a big hug.

Aunt Belle smiled. "Rosa to the rescue!" she said. Then Rosa smiled back and whispered in Aunt Belle's ear.

Aunt Belle grinned and nodded. "Wait right here," she told Oliver and his mother. Then she hurried to her chair and returned with the balloon.

"Here, Oliver," she said. "We don't really need this. Now you'll never get lost again."

"It's time for us to pack up," said Aunt Belle as Oliver and his mother went back to their umbrella. Rosa collected their things. Aunt Belle folded up her beach chair. Then they headed for the car.

While Aunt Belle directed traffic out of the parking lot, Rosa took a last look at the beach. In the water some children were finally floating on their backs. And Rosa just knew they were thinking of their belly buttons being pulled by balloons, up, up, up to the sky.